W9-CDG-963

WITHDRAWN

If your child struggles with a word, you can encourage "sounding it out," but keep in mind that not all words can be sounded out. Your child might pick up clues about a word from the picture, other words in the sentence, or any rhyming patterns. If your child struggles with a word for more than five seconds, it is usually best to simply say the word.

Most of all, remember to praise your child's efforts and keep the reading fun. After you have finished the book, ask a few questions and discuss what you have read together. Rereading this book multiple times may also be helpful for your child.

Try to keep the tips above in mind as you read together, but don't worry about doing everything right. Simply sharing the enjoyment of reading together will increase your child's reading skills and help to start your child off on a lifetime of reading enjoyment!

Frank and the Balloon

We Both Read® Book

To my kids, Jesse, Chana, and Talya, the best kids a mom could have!
—D. R.

Mom-A-Roonie, thanks for your guidance and love.
—L. R.

Text Copyright ©2007 by Dev Ross
Illustrations Copyright ©2007 Larry Reinhart
All rights reserved

We Both Read® is a trademark of Treasure Bay, Inc.

Published by
Treasure Bay, Inc.
P.O. Box 119
Novato, CA 94948 USA

Printed in Singapore

Library of Congress Catalog Card Number: 2007920850

Hardcover ISBN: 978-1-60115-011-0
Paperback ISBN: 978-1-60115-012-7

We Both Read® Books
Patent No. 5,957,693

Visit us online at:
www.webothread.com

PR 07/11

WE BOTH READ®

Frank and the Balloon

By Dev Ross

Illustrated by Larry Reinhart

TREASURE BAY

Frank the frog likes to play. He likes to play with his best friend, Mikey the mouse. One day, he and Mikey were playing on . . .

. . . the swing.

Mikey didn't want to swing too high. Swinging too high made him feel afraid, but not Frank. Frank wanted to swing up as high as he could. He wanted to swing up as high as . . .

. . . an airplane.

Frank was just thinking how fun it would be to fly in an airplane when something red whooshed past them. The red thing twirled in the air on a gust of wind, then dove out of the sky and disappeared behind some very . . .

. . . tall grass.

Frank and Mikey hurried to the grass to find the red thing. Mikey was afraid it might be something scary, but not Frank. Since it seemed to come from up in **space,** Frank was hoping the red thing was a . . .

. . . **space** man.

Frank parted the grass and saw two square eyes, a rectangular nose, and a smiling mouth, but they did not belong to a space man. The two square eyes, the rectangular nose, and the smiling mouth were painted on . . .

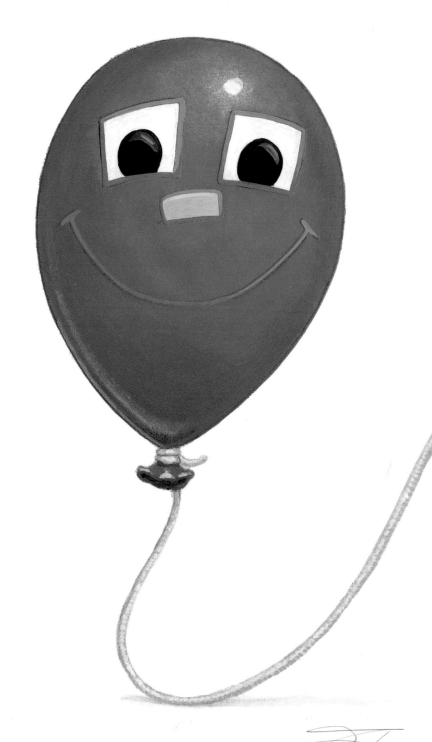

. . . a balloon.

The balloon had a long string tied to it. The string was tangled around a yellow dandelion. The tangled string was holding the balloon down. Frank untangled the string and the balloon floated . . .

. . . up!

Frank was so busy watching the balloon float up that he forgot he was holding its string. Now he was floating up too!

"Let go!" cried Mikey. He was feeling very worried for Frank. He wanted Frank to let go of the balloon's long, dangling . . .

. . . string.

Frank wanted to let go, but when he looked down he could see the ground getting further and further away. So, Frank politely asked the balloon to go down. It did not go down. Instead, it floated even higher into . . .

 . . . the sky.

From high in the sky, Frank could see wonderful things below him. He could see the pond where he lived. He could see the tops of trees. He could even see Mikey, who was his very best . . .

. . . friend.

"Come back, Frank!" shouted Mikey.

Frank, however, did not want to go back. He wanted to be the first frog to travel around the whole wide world. He wanted to be the first frog . . .

. . . to fly.

Mikey didn't want his best friend to fly. In fact, he didn't want him to stay up in the sky a single minute longer.

"Frogs should not be so high up!" Mikey scolded. "Frogs should be down here. You should . . .

. . . come down!"

⊗ "Don't worry, Mikey! I like being up here!" said Frank.

Then all of a sudden . . . WHOOSH! The balloon and Frank were carried up even higher by a blustery gust . . .

. . . of wind.

 "Whee!" cried Frank.

"Oh, no!" wailed Mikey.

"Moo!" called out another voice from below.

Frank looked down and saw that he was
floating right over Betty, . . .

. . . the cow.

Betty, the cow, was very surprised when Mikey jumped on her back.

"Follow that balloon!" roared Mikey.

Betty the cow **ran** after the balloon. **She** did not run slowly.

She ran fast!

Meanwhile, Frank said hello to a passing bird. He winked at a buzzing bumble bee. He waved at a beautiful . . .

. . . butterfly.

Then, Frank saw that he was floating further and further away from his **home**.

Suddenly, he no longer wanted to be the first frog to go around the whole wide world. He wanted only one thing. Frank wanted . . .

. . . to go **home**.

Frank climbed up to the top of the balloon and pushed and pushed. He wanted the balloon to go down. As Frank pushed, he heard the saddest cry.

"Meuw . . . Meuw . . ." Frank looked down and saw something little and furry stuck in a tree. It was . . .

. . . a kitten.

The kitten had climbed up the tree and could not get down. Now, Frank forgot all about himself. Now, all he could think about was helping the kitten. Frank climbed down the string and stretched out . . .

. . . his arms.

The kitten jumped into Frank's outstretched arms
and, together, their weight made the balloon go
down. They landed softly in the grass next to
Betty, Mikey, and a very happy little . . .

 . . . girl.

The girl thanked Frank for saving her kitten and for finding her lost balloon, and then ran happily back to her home.

Betty gave her new friends, Frank and Mikey, a ride back to their home. Mikey was pleased. He had his best friend back.

Frank and Mikey were very . . .

. . . happy.

If you liked *Frank and the Balloon*, here is another
We Both Read® Book you are sure to enjoy!

Frank, an adventurous little frog, is playing with his
friends, when suddenly his ball flies off and bounces
into the house of a giant! Frank's friends are too
scared to help him get his ball back, so he sneaks into
the huge house all by himself. There he is discovered
by the giant, who seems big and scary to Frank, but
who is really a friendly little boy.